JOEL, THE POTTER'S SON

Books by Georgiana Dorcas Ceder

ETHAN, THE SHEPHERD BOY

ANN OF BETHANY

JOEL, THE POTTER'S SON

Joel, the Potter's Son

BY GEORGIANA DORCAS CEDER

Illustrated by Helen Torrey

ABINGDON PRESS

New York • Nashville

TO MY BROTHERS

CONTENTS

Joel's little brother, Zeri, was calling

TO THE HIGHWAY

Joel and his father, Abner the potter, stood together outside the gate in the high stone wall.

"The wind blows from the east," said Abner. He lifted one hand to feel the air and nodded with satisfaction. "The sun will shine soon. The clay will dry." He went through the gate, crossed the courtyard, and disappeared into his workshop.

Left alone, Joel dug his bare toes into the path and stared at the gray December sky. The clouds were breaking, drifting westward over the green hills of Galilee toward the sea.

A sudden restlessness stirred deep within Joel. He took a few quick steps toward the road to Cana, and stopped. His little brother, Zeri, was calling.

"Joel! Joel! Father says to carry the clay pieces from the shop into the courtyard to dry in the sun."

"Always the shop and the courtyard, or the field where I lead

9

the goat," Joel grumbled as he turned back. "I wish I could go somewhere . . . somewhere far away."

"I will help you," said Zeri. He followed Joel across the court-yard to their father's pottery shop, built against the hillside.

In the corner of the shop Abner sat with his foot on the potter's wheel. It made scratchy, whirring sounds as it turned.

Nearby Cousin Seth stood at a table, kneading some clay. He smiled at Joel. "You run as fast as a turtle," he chuckled. "If you work like that, you will not make many bowls or lamps when you become a potter."

"Maybe I will not be a potter," muttered Joel. He frowned as he looked at the cups, lamps, and bowls everywhere around the shop. So many things were waiting to be carried out to be dried in the sun and then baked in the kiln.

Joel took a deep breath. "Take the small ones," he told Zeri.

"Ones like this?" asked Zeri, picking up a saucer-like lamp.

Joel nodded. He lifted a large jar to his shoulder and walked outside with it. Halfway across the courtyard he set it down beside the baking kiln which stood there, looking like a great stone beehive.

"Lift and put down with care," warned his father when Joel returned to the shop. "Leave the large jars for Seth to carry. The moist clay is heavy."

"I can take them," bragged Joel. His steps lagged as he went back and forth between shop and courtyard. Zeri trotted beside him, or darted ahead to put a cup or a lamp just where Joel expected to place the piece he carried.

After a while Joel sat down near the kiln to rest. He glanced up at the terrace on the roof over the shop. His mother, Martha, was there, grinding wheat and singing as she worked:

> " 'Bless the Lord, O my soul;
> And all that is within me, bless his holy name.' "

Zeri brought another cup from the shop.

His mother stopped singing and called out, "What are you doing, Zeri?" There were love and laughter in her voice.

"Helping Joel," answered Zeri. He stood for a moment, proud and tall for his six years, then hurried into the shop.

Martha laughed softly. "He does what he can," she said to Joel.

"Helping," grunted Joel, and stood up.

Reba, Joel's sister, came from the house back of the terrace, tying a white scarf over her smooth dark hair. "I am going to the fountain," she said to her mother. She picked up a pitcher, walked lightly down the stone steps, across the courtyard, and out the gate.

Joel followed her through the gate. He looked after her with envy, watching until she turned from the path into the road. Reba will meet her friends at the fountain in Cana, he said to himself. Why should I not go to the village too, to see mine? I will go to see Philo, at his father's shop.

A little way down the path Joel paused and started to turn back. Suddenly he changed his mind. I can carry out the rest of the clay pieces when I come home, he decided. With quick steps he walked to the road and into Cana.

In front of the shop Philo was weighing grain for a woman of the village. He nodded to Joel.

Inside, Simon, Philo's father, was tucking fresh green leaves around pomegranates and grapes piled on a tray. He beckoned to

Joel and said, "In a few weeks I go to Tyre. Tell your father if he wishes to send pottery, I will take it."

"I will tell him," Joel promised.

He watched Philo empty the grain into a clean cloth held by the woman. When she had gone, Philo took some small round sheep bones from his waistband. "See?" he said to Joel. "My father has given me some knucklebones. We could play . . ."

Philo bent down and started to make a circle on the ground, then he glanced around with keen blue eyes and said, "No . . . instead of playing, let us go to the highway at the top of the hill."

Joel thought of the clay pieces that needed to be put out in the sun and hesitated. "The highway is far," he said.

"The farther the better!" exclaimed Philo. "We would see travelers— caravans, perhaps. May I go, Father?"

"Yes, yes." Simon waved his hand. "Take the itch out of your heels." He scooped some walnuts from a large basket. "Eat these on your way."

Philo divided the nuts with Joel. They tucked them into their waistbands and started.

Beyond the village the boys left the road to follow a steep path. When they reached the top of the hill they threw themselves down on the ground, out of breath.

Philo took some nuts from his waistband and began to crack them and eat the nutmeats.

The two boys watched the people passing along the highway on foot and on donkeys. To their delight a caravan appeared. The camels stalked along, stretching their slender necks and lifting their heads high.

"They come from Tyre, I think," said Philo.

Joel nodded. "Perhaps they go to Jerusalem. Have you been there?" he asked.

"No," mumbled Philo, chewing a nut.

"I went there last spring at Passover time," said Joel. "My father took me to the Temple to become a son of the Law."

Philo looked at him and frowned. "What is that?" he asked.

"It means that I am twelve years old and have learned the laws of my people," Joel explained. "In the Temple I promised to keep the Commandments."

He sat up and clasped his hands around his knees. Philo was different, Joel remembered. Philo was Greek. He had come from Damascus a few months ago. He did not learn the Law and Commandments, or go to the synagogue on the Sabbath . . . or keep the feast days, or go to the Temple in Jerusalem.

"I would like to go to Jerusalem again next year," said Joel. "I would like to go every year."

Philo shrugged. "I shall be a merchant like my father. Some day I shall have camels and go to many cities." He cracked a nut.

"Look!" exclaimed Joel, jumping up. "Horses!"

A troop of horsemen dashed by, raising a cloud of dust.

Philo grunted and spit out a bit of nutshell. "Roman soldiers! My father says they take all the money for taxes."

Joel's eyes flashed. "They do worse. They make people slaves . . ."

A smooth voice broke in. "They do!"

Startled, Joel and Philo turned. Two strange men stood nearby.

The slender man with the thin smile spoke again. "You do not love those Romans? Nor do we." He looked after the horsemen that had passed and his eyes narrowed. "They are everywhere," he muttered. "One must always watch."

"They burn cities, and kill our men . . . our patriots," said Joel.

The slender man nodded. He turned toward his companion, a taller, heavier man. "My friend Phineas and I have heard about the men of Galilee who fought at Sepphorus. Yes . . . and we . . . we are patriots, too."

Phineas said something in a gruff voice under his breath.

Reaching out, the slender man touched Joel's waistband where the walnuts made little bulges. "You have something there, my friend? Coins, perhaps? We need food for our journey. Will you give to . . . to patriots?"

Before Joel could answer, Philo spoke. "They are not coins, only a few walnuts."

Phineas laughed harshly. "Walnuts, Jabez. Walnuts!"

Joel took some nuts from his waistband and held them out. "Take these, if you be patriots."

There was a glint in Jabez' eyes as he took the nuts.

"Come, we have far to go," he said to Phineas.

"And empty stomachs," growled the big man, as they went to the highway and started toward the east.

"Patriots!" Philo said the word with scorn.

Joel watched the men. "I think they are," he said slowly. "Did you hear the one called Jabez say they did not love the Romans? And that one must always watch? Did you see how he looked after the soldiers? I have heard my father tell how men gathered in the hills around here, lived in caves, and fought with the Romans. That was when I was little."

"I have heard of them too," said Philo. "They were brave. But those?" He shook his head. "The words of Jabez are soft, like butter. And his eyes are sharp as steel."

"They are patriots," insisted Joel. "I think they are spying on the Romans."

He would ask his father. But should he tell him of the men? His father would not like his going to the highway without permission.

Suddenly Joel remembered. He had been gone a long while. There were more clay pieces to carry into the sun . . . and the sun was going down. It was time to bring in the goat.

"We must go," he said to Philo, and led the way down the hill.

THE KNIFE

When Joel came into the courtyard, his mother looked at him silently for a moment. Her eyes flashed.

Near the shop his father stooped beside Zeri, wiping the little boy's tears. Pieces of broken pottery lay on the ground.

"You come now, when the work is done!" exclaimed his mother. "Zeri tries to help, but you . . . you . . ."

His father interrupted. "It is enough, Martha. Words will not mend the bowl, nor mold a new one."

"True! But when will Joel do his part?" she demanded.

Patiently his father answered, "When the clay is ready."

"Stone-filled clay," said Martha. She walked swiftly up the stairs to the terrace.

As Joel picked up the pieces of the broken bowl, he thought of his father's words. Am I like clay to be trodden and shaped like a cup or a lamp? he asked himself.

Zeri stood beside him. "Where did you go, Joel?" he asked.

"To Cana," answered Joel. He found a walnut left in his waistband and gave it to his little brother.

Reba brought water for the washing of hands before the evening meal. "Why did you run away?" she whispered to Joel.

"I meant to come back soon," he told her.

The family gathered around the large tray set on the floor. Martha brought a dish of hot, savory stew. The smell of meat, cooked with onions and lentils, made Joel's mouth water. He was hungry.

Abner lifted his hands, bowed his head, and prayed:

> " 'Bless the Lord, O my soul,
> And forget not all his benefits.
> Who forgiveth all thine iniquities; . . .
> Who satisfieth thy mouth with good things.' "

When they had eaten, Zeri's head nodded. His eyes closed, and he leaned against Joel.

"See how he loves you?" whispered Martha, as she put away the food and brushed up the crumbs.

Joel put his arm about Zeri.

My mother has forgotten her anger, he thought.

He glanced at his father, talking with Cousin Seth of their work. All day they had been in the shop. But he had been to the highway, seeing camels, horses, Romans, and those two strangers, Jabez and Phineas.

When his father spoke to him, Joel jumped, awakening Zeri.

His father asked again, "Where were you this afternoon?"

"With Philo," answered Joel. "His father goes to Tyre soon.

He sent word that if you want to send pottery to sell he will take it."

"Tyre," said Zeri, rubbing his eyes. "What is Tyre?"

His father smiled down at him. "Tyre is a city beside the sea. Ships come there from far-off lands. They bring silver and iron and tin and lead to exchange for purple dyes and fine linen. Tyre is a rich city." Abner turned to Martha. "Do you think they will buy our village pottery?"

"Village pottery, indeed!" cried Martha. She lifted her head with pride. "Where could they find any better? Each piece shaped perfectly, the handles strong and secure, well baked . . ." She stopped for breath.

Abner smiled. "It is good pottery, my wife, but plain."

"We might send small pieces," suggested Seth. "Lamps, and cups, and bowls."

Martha put her hand on Abner's shoulder and looked down into his face. "I think you should send. And Reba and I have woven linen. Simon might take that, too."

"He has only one donkey," said Abner, with a twinkle in his dark eyes. "But perhaps we could find another."

Tyre! thought Joel. How I should like to go there, or anywhere!

A few evenings later, while Zeri lay on his sleeping mat, Joel sat beside him, telling him a story. Suddenly a hearty voice shouted from the stairway, "Greetings! Are you at home, friend Abner?"

It was Hiram, the farmer. Back of him was his son Ezra, a tall boy with bushy red hair and a shy smile.

"I will finish the story another time," Joel promised Zeri. He greeted Ezra, and they sat down near their fathers and Seth.

The farmer's booming voice filled the room. "I hear that Simon goes to Tyre in another week or two."

Abner nodded. "He would take pottery for me, but what can he carry on the back of one donkey?"

"I came to speak of that," said Hiram. "Your wife told mine that you had need of a donkey. Let Simon take mine."

"Thank you, my friend," said Abner. He stroked his dark beard and hesitated. "But Simon may be gone for a week or more. What of your plowing? And what of the dangers on the road?"

The farmer laughed. "With my son's help, the plowing is already finished. As for dangers, the roads to the west are safe enough. Now if Simon were going to the east . . ." Hiram paused and asked his son, "What was it you heard?"

"At the fountain I heard some men talking," answered Ezra. "They said that in the hills east of the Jordan River Roman legions are fighting men of our people."

"Fighting!" exclaimed Joel. A little shiver of excitement raced up his back. Those men he had met at the highway . . . they had said they were patriots. Were they fighting?

Abner turned to Joel and spoke gravely. "Fighting is not the best way, my son. We must wait for our Deliverer to come."

"The men of Galilee have had enough of fighting," added Hiram. "It is better to sow and to reap."

Joel bent his head. His face grew warm. He would not tell his father about Jabez and Phineas.

The next two weeks were busy ones. Seth prepared the clay, and Abner molded cups, lamps, and bowls. Joel gathered wood and kept the fire burning in the kiln to bake the clay. When the

19

pottery was baked and taken from the kiln, he put straw between the pieces so they would not be marred.

The day before Simon was to leave, Joel helped his father pack the pottery in deep baskets.

"We must take care that Simon does not find broken pieces when he gets to Tyre," Abner warned.

"If I went with him, I could help," Joel suggested.

"Simon has not asked for help," said his father.

Joel swallowed hard, and looked away.

Early the next morning Ezra brought the donkey. Abner and Seth fastened the baskets on each side of the donkey's back. They tied Martha's bundle of hand-woven linen on top.

Zeri stroked the donkey's soft nose. "Poor donkey," he said. "Can you carry so much?"

"He can carry more," said Ezra smiling. "Shall I put you up there?"

Zeri stepped back of Joel. "I do not want to go."

"I do," said Joel with eagerness.

"And how would we get along without you?" asked his mother, putting her arm about his shoulders.

Abner spoke. "You may go," he said, "when you are older."

Older! The word rankled in Joel's heart as he walked with his father and Ezra to the village.

They found Simon at his shop. Two great bags of walnuts were hung across the back of his donkey.

Taking the bridles of both donkeys, Simon cried, "The sun shines. It is a good sign." He turned to Philo. "Watch the shop well until my return."

"The Lord bring you home again in safety," said Abner.

Joel helped his father pack the pottery

"And with a pocket full of denarii," Simon added, winking. He prodded his donkey to make him go.

Abner spoke to Joel. "You have worked hard, my son. You need not hurry home."

Philo was walking back and forth in the shop with an air of importance. He uncovered and covered a cask of olives. "Stay with me," he urged, when Abner had left.

Joel shook his head. He did not want to sit in the shop. He wanted to do something different, to go somewhere.

Ezra was starting back to the fields. Joel walked with him to the fountain. They stopped to drink.

"I have hoeing to do. Will you come with me?" Ezra asked.

Joel took a deep breath and stretched his arms wide. "Not today."

After Ezra had gone, Joel wondered what he could do, where he could go. The highway! He might go there again. He started, but part way up the road he saw a grove of oak trees near the top of the next hill. I will go there, he decided.

Climbing up and around, past thorns and thistles, he reached the trees. Under them the ground was soft with brown fallen leaves. He rested and then went on, along a narrow ledge that led to the other side of the hill.

Evergreen bushes grew close to the ground on the rocky hillside. Joel breathed their fragrance and broke some branches to take home. On the bushes he found hard black seeds. They looked like some his mother put in the pot with the meat. He went from bush to bush, picking the seeds and stuffing them into his waistband.

As he reached for a cluster that hung near the rocks, his foot went down, down into a hole. He pushed the branches aside to see what was there. It was an opening — a cave!

Joel broke branches to clear the entrance and went in. Glancing up, he saw that the ceiling was dark. "Smoke-blackened," he said softly. "Men used to have fires here."

Broken pottery was scattered about. An empty water jug lay on its side. Walking around, he stepped on something hard. He dug into the ground with his toes and uncovered a slender object. It was a knife, crusted with earth.

Joel rubbed the knife on his sleeve and polished it with the skirt of his tunic. He looked at it again. Why, the handle was inlaid with silver. It was a beautiful knife!

Suddenly he felt the stillness in the cave. He could hear his own breathing. Quickly he stepped outside. He put the knife in his waistband with the seeds, picked up the broken branches, and started for home.

As he went, Joel looked around several times to remember the way back to the cave — *his* cave! He felt the weight of the knife in his waistband. That was his, too. He longed to show it to someone — to Ezra, Philo, or his father. They would say, "The blade is strong. There is silver in the handle." But then they would surely ask where he had found it, and he did not want to tell anyone about his cave.

"I shall not show anyone my knife," Joel said aloud. "I will keep it always."

What, though, if it slipped from his waistband? What if someone should see it? Where could he keep it safely?

"I know!" Joel said softly. "There is a place under the loose stones back of the baking kiln where I can hide it."

Joel's little brother was at the gate. "I was watching for you," he called.

Joel gave him the branches. Zeri raced up the steps with them, singing, "See what Joel brought!"

"Myrtle!" exclaimed his mother. "How good it smells!"

Joel took the seeds from his waistband. "I picked these."

"Allspice to season our meat. Put it there," said his mother, pointing to a cup on the shelf.

"Our house will be fragrant for the Festival of Lights," she added as she placed the myrtle in a large jar. "Allspice and myrtle! You brought something more?"

Joel put his hand to his waistband. Had his mother seen the knife? "What . . . what more?" he asked.

She laughed at him over her shoulder and said gaily, "Yourself!"

THE FESTIVAL OF LIGHTS

In a week the Festival of Lights was coming. Everyone was busy. Martha and Reba cleaned the house and prepared sweetmeats and cakes. They sent Joel to gather thornbush for their baking fires.

As he climbed up and down the hillside, he thought of the cave. He longed to go there, but there was no time now. After the festival, he told himself, he would go to the cave again. Each time he passed the kiln in the courtyard, he glanced toward the spot where his knife was hidden.

In the shop, Abner and Seth made candlesticks and lamps.

Joel moved the clay pieces into the sun to dry and helped to put them in the kiln. He set the finished pottery out in the courtyard and called his father when people of the village came to buy.

The day before the festival Joel was helping his father straighten the shop. Zeri followed Joel about, getting in the way. In his hand he carried a tiny lamp his father had made for him.

"When can I light my lamp?" he asked. "When will we light all the candles and the lamps?"

"Tomorrow night," answered Joel, "when the festival begins."

"What is festival?" asked Zeri.

"A festival," said Joel, "is a . . . a feast."

"But why . . ." Zeri began.

Weary of questions, Joel said, "Ask Father."

Abner sat down and put his arm about Zeri. "Many years ago," he said, "a wicked man went into the Temple in Jerusalem. He wanted the treasures that were there — the golden candlestick, the golden lamp, the fine linen, and many other things. He took them away and built an altar there, for idols, in the Temple of the Lord.

For a few years the altar stayed there. Then Maccabeus came and fought the soldiers of the wicked man . . . "

Joel broke in. "Maccabeus was a patriot. He was brave."

"And good, too," Abner added gravely. "Maccabeus purified the Temple and lighted the fire again on the altar. Ever since then our people light candles and put lanterns on the roofs in memory of that time."

Zeri drew a long, contented breath. "Tomorrow I will help to light them," he said.

The next evening Joel went with Abner and Seth to the synagogue. When they came out from the service, lights were twinkling all over Cana. People were carrying torches and lamps and calling gay greetings to one another.

Joel and his father and Seth hurried toward home. As they turned from the road to the path, they saw lighted lanterns on the terrace over the shop. When they crossed the courtyard, they heard Martha and Reba singing.

Zeri came running down the stairs. "I helped Mother light the candles," he cried. "Six of them. One for each of us. Tomorrow night we will light more."

"Two for each of us," said Joel. He ruffed Zeri's soft hair. "Each night for eight nights there will be one more candle for each of us."

"Our whole house will be full of lights," sang Zeri.

Joel looked proudly around the room, decorated with the green myrtle branches he had brought.

On the tray, set on the floor, the feast was spread — meat and bread, cheese and goat's milk, sweet cakes, grapes, and nuts. The family gathered around it.

Joel carried the pitcher and poured water over each one's hands. Zeri followed him with a towel for wiping. In his small voice he chanted: "Bless the Lord . . ."

When they had eaten, Martha began to sing, and they all joined in. They had just finished singing a psalm when Joel heard someone call. He jumped up and ran to the door.

Simon, Philo's father, was coming up the stairway.

"Greetings," he cried, as he entered the room.

Abner stood up. "You are welcome, friend Simon. I am glad you have returned safely from Tyre." He hesitated, and added, "This is one of our feast days."

"I know," answered Simon. "I did not come to speak of business. I have news that could not wait . . . good news."

Abner motioned to a place beside him. "Sit here, friend."

Quietness filled the room like evening shadows. Everyone looked at Simon. Joel leaned forward to listen.

"It is a strange story I have to tell," said Simon. "In Tyre, in a shop near the sea, I met a man. We talked of Galilee, and I told him of the springs of water, green fields, pomegranate trees, walnuts, and olives here. Then he asked the name of my village. When I said Cana, he exclaimed, 'Do you know a potter there named Abner?' "

Martha turned to Abner. "How could he know of you?"

"Peace," said Abner gently. "Let us hear Simon's story."

Simon went on: "I answered, 'Indeed I do know a potter named Abner. Why do you ask?'

"The stranger said, 'I will tell you. I come from a city in Italy — Tarentum. I live in an inn, close to the waterfront. A woman and her daughter care for the inn. When I told them I was sailing to Tyre, the woman spoke of her brother. He lived in Cana, which she said was no great distance from Tyre. He was a potter, named Abner.' "

"My sister and her daughter!" exclaimed Abner. His deep voice trembled. "For eight years we have not known where they were. The Romans took them as slaves . . ."

Simon interrupted. "They are slaves no longer. The stranger from Tarentum said that the man who bought them owned the inn. He gave them their freedom and left the inn to them when he died."

His father's sister? Seth's mother! Joel looked at Seth. His eyes were shining. He was scarcely breathing.

Joel glanced at his mother. She was rocking herself from side to side and whispering solemnly:

"'Bless the Lord, O my soul, . . .
Who redeemeth thy life from destruction;
Who crowneth thee with lovingkindness . . .
As the heaven is high above the earth,
So great is his mercy . . .' "

Simon stood up. "I came quickly to bring you the news," he said. "I left the donkey with Hiram on my way. Tomorrow I will return to tell you about our business."

Abner rose, too. He clasped Simon's hand. "Our hearts are full of thanks for your words. It is a day of rejoicing."

The candles flickered. Joel turned around. Six candles burning, one for each of them. No! Reba was lighting two more. One each for the mother and sister of Seth!

The next day, when Simon came back, Joel listened eagerly as he talked with Abner about the journey.

"The merchants of Tyre liked your pottery and the linen,"

said Simon. "If you wish, I will take more for you when I go again. In about two months I will take pomegranate bark for the dye-makers."

"We will send pottery and linen," agreed Abner.

In the evening more candles were lighted. Candles, too, for Seth's mother and sister in Italy.

"Will they come here?" Joel asked.

Abner shook his head. "It would cost too much, and they are well settled."

"I might go to them," suggested Seth.

"That, too, would cost much," said Abner. He added thoughtfully, "But a man might get work on a ship . . . help to load and unload. You might talk with Simon about it."

Joel stared at Seth. Would he really go on a ship, over the sea? I would not like that, thought Joel, but I would like to go to Tyre. Maybe I could go with Simon next time. I might ask him. If he said yes, I could ask my father. Surely then he would let me go. Joel's face grew warm as he dreamed about it. He would be no trouble to Simon. He would help with the donkeys. And he would take his knife, in case of danger.

The Festival of Lights lasted for eight days. After that everyone slipped back into his usual round of work.

Each day Joel took the goat to the field. Each day he brought back wood for the fires and stacked it near the kiln. Sometimes, when no one was looking, he lifted the stones where his knife was hidden. He rubbed it to make it shine, admired it, and hid it again.

One morning Abner said, "The clay is almost gone. We must go to the pit for more."

They borrowed Hiram's donkey to carry the baskets. Joel

helped to load the baskets and shovels on the donkey's back. With his father and Seth he walked down the hillside to the pit.

While Abner and Seth dug and filled the baskets with clay, Joel led the donkey to a little stream to drink. He thought about his cave and wished it were nearer, so he could go there again.

When he returned, he heard his cousin saying, "Who will help in the shop, if I should go?"

"It is time for Joel to begin," answered Abner.

At the end of the day, when the last load of clay was piled against the wall in the shop, Joel led the donkey back to Hiram's. On his way home he stopped to see Philo. Seth was there, talking with Simon.

"Let us play knucklebones," Philo suggested. "I have been practicing." He marked a circle on the ground and placed a row of knucklebones across it. Kneeling a little way off, he doubled his fist, aimed, and shot a larger bone toward those in the circle. Several of the small bones rolled out of line.

Philo looked up, smiling. "Can you do as well? Here is a knucklebone. Try it."

Joel knelt down, but his thoughts were not on the game. He was listening to Simon as he said to Seth, "The first of March I go to Tyre. Come with me and I will help you find a ship."

Philo nudged Joel. "Why do you wait?"

"I do not want to play," said Joel. He flung the knucklebone on the ground and walked away from the shop. Angry thoughts raced through his mind. He wanted to go to Tyre with Simon. If Seth went, his father would not let him go, he knew.

When Seth caught up with him, Joel blurted out his question. "Will you go to Tyre with Simon?"

"Yes," answered Seth, "I will go."

Joel muttered, "I wanted to go this time."

"But you are needed here!" exclaimed Seth.

Needed! Joel's heart was filled with resentment. He kicked a stone from the road and walked on without speaking.

As they sat on the terrace that evening, Seth told Abner and Martha he would go to Tyre with Simon early in March. He would find a ship sailing to Italy.

"It is right," said Abner. "You will bring joy to your mother and sister."

"Who will work with you in the shop?" asked Martha.

Abner answered quietly, "Our son will help."

A lump came into Joel's throat. Help! Stay, when he wanted to go! He left the terrace and went to his sleeping mat.

A few days later Abner washed the little stones from the clay. He placed a small pile of it on a large flat rock in the shop. He called Joel and said, "It is time for you to tread."

Joel tucked up his tunic. For a moment he stood on the wet clay. Then he lifted one foot after the other and brought each down hard, pressing the moisture and air out of the clay. Up, down! Up, down! The minutes dragged. Joel's legs ached.

My feet go, but they take me nowhere, Joel said to himself. But Seth . . . Seth is going to Tyre — and farther. As far as Italy. Joel's feet moved slower and slower.

Abner finished molding a dish. He came to Joel and said, "Rest now, my son. I will tread."

Joel squatted in the sunshine beside the door, watching his father. It took long to prepare the clay. Was it easier to shape it? Some day he would try.

Early and late through the dark, rainy month of January the whir of the potter's wheel sounded in the shop. Abner and Seth worked steadily, and Joel helped. In February, between showers, the clay was fired.

The weeks slipped by. There was a smell of summer on the way the day Hiram's donkey was brought again, to be loaded with pottery and linen. And it was time for Seth to go. Martha, Reba, and Zeri hugged him and bade him good-by.

"Joel and I will walk with you a little way," said Abner. His voice was husky.

They found Simon waiting for them at his shop in Cana. Simon's donkey was loaded with great bundles of pomegranate bark.

He led the way with the two donkeys. Seth walked after him, between Abner and Joel.

Near the next village Abner stopped. "Joel and I must turn back here," he said. Placing his hand on Seth's bowed head, he prayed: "The Lord bless thee and make thee a blessing."

Seth answered: " 'The Lord watch between me and thee.' "

He turned, put his hand on Joel's shoulder, and smiled. "You will take my place now, in the shop."

Joel watched, a sudden ache in his throat, as Seth walked up the hill after Simon.

STUBBORN CLAY

The air was soft. Blossoming apricot trees made white patches against the dark green of the fields. In the quiet of the evening Joel sat with the rest of the family on the roof.

"I wonder where Seth is," murmered Reba.

Martha sighed. "Perhaps on the sea. It is two weeks since he left us."

Joel missed Seth, too. More than once he had looked up, expecting to see him, and then remembered.

Seth was gone, and he was left — left to work in the shop. The muscles in his legs ached, though he knew they grew stronger each day. He could work the clay with his feet for a much longer time than when he first began. Still he could not do as much as Seth.

"You do well," Abner told Joel one morning, "But it takes weight to press the air from the clay. That will come."

Abner put a lump of clay on the wheel. He pushed the lower

wheel with his foot, and the upper wheel turned with it. Beneath his skillful hands the clay became a tall, smooth jar.

"One must learn the feel of the clay to know when it is right for shaping," he said. Taking a piece of rope, he wound it tightly around the jar and pressed it against the clay. When he took it off, the twisted mark of the rope was left in the clay. He took more clay, shaped small handles, and fastened one on each side of the jar.

Joel admired the jar. Rich people in Tyre would surely want to buy it. He picked up a bit of clay and rubbed it between his fingers. Was it right for shaping? he wondered.

Reba brushed past him into the shop. "The tax collector has come to Cana," she gasped. "It is not the one who came last year, but a stranger. He has a parchment roll with the names of the people of Cana written on it, and the tax each must pay."

Carefully Abner lifted the jar from his wheel and set it on the ground nearby. "I will go and find out about our tax."

"I will go too," said Joel.

"No," said his father. "You stay here. Watch the shop and do what you can."

"Stay, always stay!" grumbled Joel when his father had gone.

"The goat is crying," said Zeri, coming into the shop.

Joel spoke to him sharply. "Father told you to take her to the field in the morning and bring her back at night. That is your part, now that Seth is gone. I had work to do here." He glanced around. "I may make a cup . . . or a lamp," he added.

Zeri's eyes opened wide. "On the wheel?"

"Why not?" bragged Joel. He had never tried it, but he knew how it worked. He sat down beside the wheel. Excitement flowed through him.

35

Taking a lump of clay, he rolled it between his palms and placed it on the center of the upper wheel. He cupped his hands around it and shoved the lower wheel with his foot. The wheels moved with a gritty whir, slowly, then faster. Suddenly the clay beneath Joel's hands sprang upward, as though it were alive. He clutched it and stopped the wheel.

"That is not a cup," said Zeri. "That is a . . . a post."

Joel tried again. He tried several times. It looked easy, but he could not shape the clay.

"When Father turns the wheel, it goes the way he wants it to go," remarked Zeri.

Joel frowned. "It is the clay," he said. He rubbed a bit of it between his fingers. The clay always obeyed the touch of his father's hands. But to him it seemed to say: *I will go this way . . . not that way.* It was stubborn clay!

Zeri was watching him.

On the ground near the wheel stood the jar Abner had just shaped. Joel lifted it and placed it on the wheel. He pushed the lower wheel, pretending he had shaped the jar. The upper wheel spun around. The jar slipped through Joel's hands and fell to the ground with a dull thud. Joel caught his breath.

"What will Father say?" cried Zeri. "You spoiled . . . "

"Keep still," ordered Joel. He picked up the jar. One side was flattened where it had fallen.

"Can you fix it?" whispered Zeri.

Joel's hands fumbled as he pressed the clay, trying to straighten the jar. It leaned to one side and would not stand when he tried to set it on the ground.

"What will you do?" asked Zeri.

36

It looked easy, but Joel could not shape the clay

"Do!" exclaimed Joel. "The goat is crying. I will take her out. You can stay and watch the shop."

Joel walked quickly to the goat's pen back of the stairway. He put a chain around the animal's neck and led her away as fast as she would go. Several times he glanced around to see if Zeri were following him, or if his father were coming back.

After the goat had a drink at the spring, Joel led her on to the field. He fastened the chain to a tree stump and sat down, thinking about the jar. His father had told him to stay in the shop, but he did not want to return . . . yet. Zeri was there, he argued within himself. Zeri could call his mother if anyone came.

Joel began to think of the cave he had found. I will go there now, he decided. I found my knife there. I might find something more.

He started up the hill. Olive and pomegranate trees were in blossom. Scarlet anemones nodded in the sun. Farther on, a lark flew up, singing. Joel stopped to listen.

Someone called, and he glanced back. A small boy was coming slowly up the hill. It was Zeri.

Joel waved his hand. "Go home!" he shouted.

His little brother kept plodding up the hill toward him.

"What do you want?" Joel called out.

Zeri did not answer. When he reached Joel, he sat down, out of breath.

"Did Father come?" asked Joel. "Did he send you for me?"

"He did not come and you did not come," answered Zeri. "So I came to find you."

"You cannot come with me," Joel said with sharpness.

A hurt look came into Zeri's dark eyes. "Why?"

"Because you cannot walk so far," answered Joel.

Zeri's lips quivered. "Most every day I walk with the goat."

Joel wiggled his toes in the cool grass. He did not want to go back, but if Zeri went home someone would ask, "Where is Joel?" And Zeri would tell them.

"You spoil everything. If you had not been watching, the jar might not have slipped," Joel said under his breath. He looked toward the oak trees high on the next hill. Could Zeri walk that far and then wait while he went on to the cave?

"Come, if you must," he said.

He slowed his steps to those of Zeri. When they came to a little stream, Zeri wanted a drink. They cupped their hands to catch the drops. They cooled their feet in the water and went on.

At last they reached the oak grove. Zeri lay down with a sigh, too tired to go farther.

"Stay here," said Joel. "I will come back soon."

Zeri sat up. "Take me with you," he pleaded, glancing around. "Foxes might come or . . . "

"Afraid of little foxes that come at night to steal the grapes?" asked Joel. Then he frowned. There were jackals in the hills, and sometimes a wolf. He could not leave Zeri here alone. But even if Zeri were not tired, the cave was a secret. Joel did not want to share it with anyone.

He sat down, picked up a brown leaf and tore it to little pieces. They would have to go back . . . back to the shop, as soon as Zeri was rested. Some other day he would try to slip away from Zeri and go to the cave.

Trudging downhill was easier than climbing up, but it was a long walk back.

On their way Joel picked up a large piece of wood. "This will burn well in the kiln," he said. Perhaps, he thought, when my father sees it he will not be so angry.

Zeri stumbled along. Joel's feet lagged, too, as they drew near home.

At the gate he took a quick glance around. He could smell the fresh-baked bread his mother was taking from the oven. He could see Reba at her loom on the roof. From the shop came the buzz of the wheel. His father was working.

Zeri plumped down on the first step. Joel carried the piece of wood past the workshop to the corner of the courtyard. The buzz of the wheel stopped. Abner called.

Joel's heart beat fast as he stepped into the shop. He looked at his father, then down at the ground, and waited.

"What have you to say?" Abner's voice was stern.

"I . . ." Joel swallowed. "I am sorry. The jar slipped."

"I can make another, though it takes much time to prepare the clay," said Abner, "but there is something more."

Joel shifted uneasily from one foot to the other.

"You spoiled the jar," said Abner. "Then you went away."

"I took the goat to the field," said Joel. "I told Zeri . . ."

His father interrupted. "Zeri has nothing to do with it. I bade you stay in the shop." In a low, grave voice he added, "You disobeyed, my son. Do not let it happen again."

WILL WE GO?

Stay in the shop! Stay, always stay!

I wish I could go away and never come back! thought Joel.

As he went into the courtyard, Reba called to him. "Did you bring the goat home?"

Joel started to say, "That is Zeri's work." He glanced at his little brother, asleep on the step. "I will get her," he muttered.

He was loosening the goat's chain from the stump of the tree when he heard a sharp whistle. It was Ezra. Joel went to meet him.

Walking along the road Ezra said, "The barley is growing fast. It will be ready for harvest by the time we return from Jerusalem."

"Jerusalem!" exclaimed Joel.

"For the Passover," added Ezra. "Have you forgotten? It comes the week after next."

"You went last year, too," said Joel.

Ezra nodded. "Are you going?"

"My father has not spoken of it," answered Joel. "But yes. Yes, I think we will go."

"Then we can walk together, as we did last year," said Ezra. He left Joel at the turn in the road.

"Jerusalem!" The name made Joel's heart thump. Surely they would go. His father had not thought to mention it because of Seth's going and the tax collector's coming. Joel hurried home.

He was putting the goat in the pen when Reba came to do the milking. "I met Ezra," Joel told her. "He is going to Jerusalem for the Passover. I am going . . ."

Reba broke in. "We went last year."

"So did Ezra," said Joel. "And he went the year before."

"Because his married sister lives there," said Reba, starting to milk. "But everyone in the village cannot go to Jerusalem every year."

Joel left the goat's pen. Should he ask his father now? No. Tonight it would be better for Zeri to ask.

His little brother lay asleep on the step. "Wake up! Come," Joel whispered, and led the way up the stairs.

On the terrace Martha was stirring beans in a clay pot over the fire. Joel took Zeri's hand. They went on up to the roof.

"The Feast of the Passover is coming," said Joel. "Do you want to go to Jerusalem?"

"My legs are tired," said Zeri, still half asleep.

"Remember last year we went with Ezra and Hiram, and they let you ride the donkey when you were tired?" asked Joel.

Zeri nodded and yawned.

"Remember the people?" said Joel. "And how they shouted when they saw Jerusalem? And Father lifted you up so you could see the walls of the city and the towers and the Temple?"

Zeri closed his eyes and rested his head on one fist.

Joel shook him a little to wake him and said, "Ask Father if we will go to Jerusalem again this year."

"Will I ride the donkey?" asked Zeri.

"Zeri! Joel!" Martha called. "Come! Wash and eat."

"Ask Father about Passover," Joel whispered to Zeri as they gathered around the tray.

Zeri fell asleep while he was eating. As Abner picked him up to hold him, Zeri opened his eyes. "The Feast of the Passover is coming," he murmured.

Joel held his breath. He watched his father, and waited.

"It is indeed," said Abner. He smiled with tenderness at Zeri. "We will not forget it. We will keep the Passover, work, and pay the tax collector, until our Deliverer comes."

"Will . . . " Joel began, then paused. He wanted to ask, *Will we go to Jerusalem?* Instead he said, "Will our Deliverer be king, instead of Herod?"

Abner spoke thoughtfully. "We must wait and see. He will lead us in paths we have not known. He will make darkness light before us . . . and crooked things straight."

A little shiver of excitement spread down Joel's back. We are going! Going to Jerusalem! My father would not speak so if he did not mean that. To go to Jerusalem for the feast is much better than to go to Tyre.

Plans for the journey to Jerusalem filled Joel's thoughts as he worked in the shop the next few days. He hummed as he worked. His feet were sure and hard as he trod the clay.

Then Simon came, and work stopped. Martha left her grind-

ing and Reba her loom. They gathered around Simon on the terrace.

"First tell us of Seth," begged Martha. "Did he find a ship?"

"Yes," answered Simon with a smile. "He found a Roman galley with two rows of men at the oars and sails beside. They will go swiftly. Seth helped to load the ship with spices and silks to pay for his passage. Now I must speak of our business."

Simon drew his moneybag from his waistband. As he gave Abner his share of the money from the sale of the pottery, Hiram came.

"Welcome home!" Hiram greeted Simon heartily. "I heard in the village you had returned. Tell us the news from Tyre."

Martha and Reba slipped away to their work. Joel edged nearer to listen.

Simon answered, "They say the emperor has ordered the ruler of Jerusalem to come to Rome. A Roman governor has been sent to take the ruler's place. There has been much trouble in Judea and in Jerusalem these past few years."

"True," said Hiram. "My daughter lives there. I shall go there soon for the Passover. I will hear more about it then."

Joel nodded. I will go, too, he thought.

"I saw ships bringing more Roman legions," said Simon. "I am glad to be safe in Cana."

"You fear there may be trouble?" asked Hiram, frowning. "What do you think, friend Abner? Will you go with us to Jerusalem for the Passover this year?"

Joel smiled, waiting for his father's word.

"No," said Abner gravely. "We will not go this year."

The singing that had been in Joel's heart stopped. Not go? He stared at his father.

Joel walked away from the men, down the steps and into the shop. "We will not go this year!" The words sounded over and over in his ears.

When Simon and Hiram left, Abner returned to his work.

Joel went to the kneading table where his father pressed and rolled the clay back and forth.

"What is it, my son?" asked his father.

It was hard for Joel to speak. "You said . . . you said we will not go. Hiram and Ezra are going. Why . . . "

Abner stopped kneading. "We cannot afford to go. I gave all the money I could to Seth when he left. It was little enough. He had worked hard and long. He had earned it."

"But Simon gave you money today," said Joel.

45

"He did," agreed Abner. "But the tax collector took twice as much as he did last year." Abner paused, and a shadow passed over his face. "I had to borrow from Hiram to pay the tax. When I repay him there will be little left. The making of pottery is slow work. It would take a week, or more, to go to Jerusalem for the feast. I cannot spare that much time."

Joel was silent for a moment. "Could I go . . . with Ezra and Hiram?" he asked.

His father answered with firmness, "It is better not to go this year. You heard what Simon said today? These are troubled times in Judea and in Jerusalem. And I need you here."

"But I — " Joel gulped — "I am a son of the Law."

"A son of the Law is a son anywhere." Abner's voice was gentle. "I am sorry for your disappointment. We will go another year. You cannot go this year." He began to work again. "See if the fire is burning well under the kiln."

Joel went about his work, but his mind was filled with rebellious thoughts. His father did not want to let him go! "All he wants me to do is stay . . . and work," muttered Joel.

The same thoughts burned in Joel's heart during the days that followed. He hardly spoke to anyone. When it grew too dark to work in the shop, he would slip away and walk to the fountain in Cana. There he listened to the villagers, planning their pilgrimage. Ezra and the other boys talked only of going to Jerusalem.

One day Joel saw Reba near the place where his knife was hidden. He called out rudely, "What are you doing there?"

"Taking some wood," answered Reba. "Why are you so cross? What is the matter with you?"

Joel did not answer. At his first chance he took his knife from its hiding place. He would carry it in his waistband until he found a safer place for it.

At last the day came for the pilgrims to start. Joel went with his father and mother, Reba, and Zeri, to wish their friends a safe journey.

It seemed as though all the people of Cana had gathered in the market place. There were donkeys and carts loaded with tents, sleeping mats, and baskets of food for the journey.

The morning was half gone before everything was ready and the pilgrims started on their way, like a procession, up the road to the highway.

The people left behind shouted and waved.

"Come along," Ezra called gaily to Joel. "Walk with us part of the way."

"Go," said Abner with a smile. "Walk as far as the highway, if you wish."

Joel ran to catch up with Ezra. If only he were going all the way! At least he could pretend that he was going, until he reached the highway.

A BASKET OF FOOD

The pilgrims walked slowly up the hill beside their loaded donkeys and carts. The heavy wheels of the carts creaked and groaned. Someone started to sing a psalm. Soon many voices were singing:

> " 'I was glad when they said to me,
>   Let us go into the house of the Lord.
>   Our feet shall stand within thy gates, O Jerusalem.' "

"I wish I were going," said Joel.

"Perhaps next year . . . " Ezra began.

Joel broke in. "What good is next year? I want to go now!"

At each village along the road more pilgrims joined the procession. It was midday when they reached the highway at the top of the hill. There they stopped to eat and drink.

Ezra shared his lunch with Joel. The bread seemed to stick

in Joel's throat. It was time for him to go back to Cana.

"While they pack their baskets, let us walk on ahead a little way," suggested Ezra.

Joel hesitated. "My father said, 'as far as the highway.' "

"You could go as far as the road that leads up from Nazareth," urged Ezra.

Joel thought for a moment. "I will go," he said, "but only that far. When I start for home I will walk fast."

They followed the highway along the top of the hill.

"Look!" Ezra pointed down a road to the south. "The people from Nazareth are coming." He glanced ahead. "See that rock at the edge of the highway? I will race you there!"

Joel ran as fast as he could, but Ezra's legs were longer. They climbed the bank beside the road and sat down, panting and laughing, to watch the people as they came along.

There were joyous greetings when friends from Nazareth, Cana, and other small villages met. In little groups they walked eastward, along the road that crossed the plain of Esdraelon, toward the city of Beth-shan.

Watching the procession, Joel and Ezra lingered on the bank above the highway. "How far will you walk today?" Joel asked.

"I think we will cross the Jordan River and put up our tents near it," Ezra answered. "Tomorrow night we should be at Jericho, and the next day . . ."

Joel interrupted. "I know! The next day you will climb the Mount of Olives. You will see Jerusalem!" He remembered how it had looked last year, and how his family had found a place for their tent on the hillside, facing toward the city.

Ezra's family was far ahead now. The groups of pilgrims were smaller and farther apart. Travelers came, going in the opposite direction.

"I must go home now," said Joel.

"And I must run after my father," said Ezra. "When I come back I will tell you all that happens." He jumped down to the road, raced along it, and was soon out of sight around a curve.

I could have gone, too, thought Joel resentfully. I could have taken care of myself. He rubbed the back of his hand over his eyes, slid down the bank, and took a few steps toward home.

What was that muffled, pounding sound? He glanced back. A troop of horsemen — Roman soldiers — galloped around the curve in the road. They were almost upon him before Joel thought to move. Stepping backward, he tripped and fell. The horse nearest to him reared, turned, and pranced while the others swept by.

As the man on the plunging horse leaned back and jerked the reins something slipped from his belt and fell unnoticed in the soft dust of the road.

Joel pointed and shouted, "Your bag!"

The man looked down, backed his horse, and motioned to Joel to hand the moneybag to him.

Joel picked it up. Then, afraid of the pawing hoofs of the horse, he edged away.

With a frown the Roman commanded, "Come nearer!"

Joel hesitated, stepped forward, and held out the bag.

The Roman took it. "Trembling rabbit!" he muttered, looking down. He opened the bag and took out a coin. Flinging it toward Joel, he spurred his horse and galloped off.

Joel stared after him. A rabbit, the Roman had called him! His face burned. With one toe he scratched around in the dust and found the coin. He did not want to touch it. Still, it would help to pay the tax collector. He picked it up, put it in his waistband, and started for home.

As he walked on, Joel saw a basket on the ground beside the road. There was no one in sight, except two or three people with a donkey coming from Nazareth. He went to look at the basket and lifted the clean cloth that covered it.

"Food!" exclaimed Joel. "Food for the journey!" The basket had dropped from a pilgrim's cart, he guessed.

Below the cloth were sweet cakes and bread, raisins and dates. Under another cloth he found cheese, olives, pieces of roasted meat, and a covered dish filled with tiny salted fish. His mouth watered.

"Someone will have no food," he said aloud. "I will run after Ezra, and give the basket to him. He can find the owner."

Joel lifted the basket. It was heavy. He ran down the road a little way, then shifted the basket to his other hand. Half running and half walking, he hurried along.

When he was out of breath, he put down the basket and paused to rest.

The last group of pilgrims, and even Ezra, were still out of sight. They must be around another bend in the highway, thought Joel. He picked up the basket and started on.

He went fast at first, then slower, and even more slowly. At last he stopped. Far ahead, in the distance, a cloud of dust hung over the road. That must be where the pilgrims walked.

Joel stepped off the road and sat down. He glanced at the sky. The sun was slanting toward the western hills. He was a long way from home. It would be late before he could get back to Cana. But what should he do about the basket? If only some other pilgrims

would come along, he could give it to them and ask them to find the owner.

Standing up, he squinted his eyes against the sun to look back. Yes . . . the people he had seen on the Nazareth road were coming.

Suddenly someone from behind him grasped his arms, pinned them to his sides, and held him tightly.

Joel struggled to free himself, twisting and turning. "Let me go!" he gasped. He looked up, then exclaimed, "Oh, it is you, Phineas!"

The big man stared and loosened his hold. Joel slipped away. Back of Phineas he saw another man. It was Jabez.

Joel rubbed his arms. "You grabbed me hard, Phineas."

"Who are you?" asked Jabez in his soft voice. He studied Joel through half-closed eyes. "We have met before?"

"Yes," answered Joel. "Have you forgotten? On the highway last winter. You talked with my friend and me. You said you were patriots . . . you did not love the Romans."

"The Romans," murmured Jabez. He lifted a slender brown finger and glanced around. "The Romans . . . yes . . ."

"I gave you some of my walnuts," Joel added.

"Walnuts, Phineas! Our young friend Walnuts! Remember him?" Jabez smiled. He patted Joel on the shoulder. "You helped us then, and now you can help again."

"Bah!" snorted Phineas. "How . . ."

Jabez interrupted. "You will see. You should be more careful not to hurt our friends." He turned to Joel. "Phineas does not know how strong he is. He only meant to startle you. You see, someone was coming to meet us . . ." Jabez paused. "Someone . . . with a basket, like yours."

"It is . . ." Joel began. He meant to say, *It is not my basket. It belongs to some pilgrim.* But Jabez broke in.

"Yes, I know. It holds food for your journey. But why will you walk alone? Your pilgrim friends are far ahead. As you said, we are patriots. We go to Jerusalem—" he lowered his voice— "to spy on the Romans. We will go together."

Phineas muttered, "People are coming."

Jabez glanced around quickly, and Joel looked, too.

While they had been talking, three people had drawn near. A tall, gray-bearded man led a donkey. A woman rode it. Beside her walked a boy in a clean white tunic. He was about as tall as Joel.

"They are from Nazareth," said Joel. "I saw them coming up the road."

Jabez nodded. "That must be Joseph, the carpenter," he said

53

to Phineas. "I heard a pilgrim ask for him, and another say that a farmer had brought in a broken yoke and that Joseph stayed to mend it."

Pilgrims! They might find the owner of the basket. Joel hesitated. Should he give it to them, or to Jabez and Phineas?

The boy's eyes met Joel's as he drew near.

"Peace," said the boy from Nazareth.

"Peace," answered Joel. A still feeling came over him. Does he know me? Joel took a step toward the highway, after the other boy.

Jabez put his hand on Joel's arm and drew him back.

"We are hungry," said Jabez. "Let us share the food in your basket."

Joel was hungry, too. He had walked most of the day and had eaten only a little of Ezra's lunch at noon. This was not his basket, but how could he ever hope to find its owner among all the pilgrims? Jabez and Phineas were patriots. Surely the owner would want to share the food with them.

Joel sat down and lifted the cloth from the basket.

Jabez looked at the food and smiled with satisfaction. "There is enough for all of us, until we reach Jerusalem," he said.

Joel took a deep breath. "I must go . . ." he began. He meant to say, *I must go home, back to Cana.* But Jabez interrupted him.

"Yes, we must go quickly, when we have eaten. Soon it will be dark. It is not too far to the inn in Beth-shan. I think we can sleep there." A queer little smile came into Jabez' eyes when Phineas grunted.

"Beth-shan," murmured Joel. He glanced toward the west. The sun had disappeared. Should he start for home, alone on the highway, in the dark? He might lose his way . . . it would be safer to go on, to the inn, just for the night. His father would want him to do that.

But what would his father and mother think when he did not return? They will believe I have gone on with Ezra, Joel decided. Tomorrow, when I get home, I will tell them how it happened.

When they had eaten, Joel picked up the basket and walked down the highway with Jabez and Phineas.

At first the basket did not seem heavy. After a while Joel's arm grew numb. He shifted the basket to his other arm.

Stars came out before they saw the flickering lights of Beth-shan. Along the road pilgrims had set up their little tents. There were tents, too, around the inn.

"No room, no room," cried the innkeeper when he saw them.

Jabez rested his hand on Joel's shoulder. "We have walked far," he said. "The boy is tired."

The innkeeper grunted. "Everyone has walked far. Everyone is tired." He looked at Joel and shrugged. "If you can find a corner . . ."

"Go in," whispered Jabez to Joel. "Find a place. We will follow."

Joel worked his way into the crowd. Close to the wall, near the door, he found room for the basket. He wedged in beside it and lay down with his arm hooked through the handle.

Something in his waistband pressed hard against him. It was his knife, and the coin, he remembered as he fell asleep.

ON TO JERUSALEM

Someone was trying to take the basket, Joel dreamed. Or was it a dream? Someone was tugging at the handle! He sat up, only half awake. A dark figure bent over him. It was Jabez.

"Bring the basket. Be silent. Come," Jabez whispered.

It was hard to see with only a night lamp burning. Joel stumbled and almost fell over another sleeper. Jabez took his arm, guided him to the door, and opened it quietly.

Before it closed, it swung open again. The innkeeper came out and called, "You go without paying?"

"Did I forget to pay last night?" exclaimed Jabez. He turned to Phineas and said, "Take care of it."

Jabez grasped the handle of the basket. "We must hurry," he said to Joel. He walked swiftly around the first corner, and hurried along the narrow street, pulling Joel with him.

"Where are we going?" mumbled Joel, his eyes half open.

Jabez did not answer. His head was turned, looking back.

"You settled . . . everything?" he asked when the big man caught up with them.

"All," answered Phineas, breathless from running. He held up a moneybag for Jabez to see before he tucked it into his waistband.

Joel blinked his eyes and asked, "Where are we?"

"We are passing through the Gap of Jezreel," answered Jabez. "Soon we will cross the Jordan River and turn south. By tomorrow night we will be in Jerusalem."

"But . . . but . . . no!" cried Joel.

"You are still dreaming," said Jabez. He hustled Joel along with the basket.

It was beginning to be light. Along the river pilgrims were folding their tents and loading their donkeys and carts.

"I must go home," Joel began again. "My father said . . ." He stopped. He did not want to tell Jabez and Phineas that his father had said, "You cannot go."

"What did your father say?" asked Jabez.

Joel answered, "My father said, 'These are troubled times.' "

"You are afraid?" exclaimed Jabez. "You are safe with us. You cannot turn back now."

"I am not afraid," said Joel. He argued within himself as he walked on between Jabez and Phineas. His father had said, "You cannot go." But he wanted to go! He had come a day's journey, and there was food in the basket. His father needed him in the shop . . . but he would not be gone long — only a few days.

The sun rose higher. Pilgrims moved along the highway, singing as they walked. Camels padded alongside the road. Horses

pranced by, tossing their heads and whinnying. Dust kicked up by many feet rose like gray clouds. Excitement, as well as dust, filled the air.

"I am thirsty," said Joel. He was hungry, too. The basket he was carrying seemed to grow heavier. But Jabez and Phineas did not stop. It was nearly noon before Jabez led the way to a little stream to drink. They sat under some palm trees and ate some bread and olives from the basket.

It was pleasant to sit in the shade. Joel would have liked to rest longer, but Phineas growled, "The highway grows crowded. Will we sit here all day?"

"We will go," said Jabez. "If we are separated," he said to Joel, "stay with Phineas until I find you again."

The big man snorted.

Phineas does not like me, thought Joel. Jabez is my friend.

People thronged the highway. Suddenly Jabez was gone.

"Jabez! Jabez!" Joel shouted. Phineas pushed him forward and muttered in his ear, "Stop shouting. He will return."

Joel looked anxiously from side to side until he caught a glimpse of Jabez in the thick of the crowd.

When he came near, Jabez smiled and nodded. Several times he disappeared and returned. Once, just after he came back, there was shouting and some disturbance in the procession back of them. Joel listened. Someone was crying, "Thieves!"

Joel tried to turn around, but Phineas pushed him along. "Take care of the basket," the big man said gruffly.

All day they walked. That evening they ate more of the food from the basket and lay down to sleep under some balsam trees.

Before he fell asleep, Joel thought about his father and mother. They would be wondering where he was. They would think he had gone with Ezra and the others to Jerusalem. They might worry. . . . Zeri would watch for him at the gate. He should go back. Tomorrow he must tell Jabez he had to go . . .

When Joel wakened, the sky was gray. He thought he had not been asleep. The night had gone fast.

Jabez was saying, "With him, we are safe. It will be as it was at Beth-shan."

Then came Phineas' harsh voice, "Someone may remember our faces. There is danger . . ."

Jabez put up his hand to silence Phineas as Joel sat up.

A little shiver ran down Joel's back. Jabez and Phineas were speaking of watching the Romans, spying!

"Let us eat before we start," said Jabez.

There was enough food for another meal, thought Joel when he covered the basket.

They joined the crowd on the highway, crossed the Jordan River again, and passed through Jericho. The road wound through brown, stony hills. There were no trees for shade and no water until they came to the spring called En Shemish. Many of the pilgrims stopped there to drink and to fill their water jugs.

Jabez, Phineas, and Joel stopped to drink, too. Then they followed the road upward, around the Mount of Olives and through the village of Bethany.

Farther on, Joel saw the city of Jerusalem — first the golden dome of the Temple, then the high towers, and at last the great walls.

The pilgrims began to shout and to sing. Joel wondered why Jabez and Phineas did not join in. The songs and the shouts made him tingle all over. He forgot his father and Cana. He was glad he had come to Jerusalem for the Passover! Joel shouted and sang, too: " 'Our feet shall stand within thy gates . . .' "

On the hillside, pilgrims were unfolding their tents.

"Last year my father pitched our tent on this hill," Joel told Jabez and Phineas. "Where will we sleep tonight?"

"We go to an inn," Jabez told him.

They crossed the bridge from the Mount of Olives to the portico along the eastern side of the Temple. Joel looked up at the great white marble columns. "I remember," he said. "This is the Porch of Solomon." Gray-bearded men sat there. They were the wise teachers of the Law, his father had told him.

Joel turned his head from side to side, wanting to see everything, until Jabez spoke to him sharply.

"It grows late. Tomorrow you can return and look."

They crossed a corner of the large court, the Court of the

Gentiles, and passed through the Temple market place. Pushing their way through its crowds, they went on, to the lower part of the city.

When they came to an inn, Phineas pounded on the door. It did not open. They tried another inn, and another. There was no room anywhere! "Where shall we sleep?" he grumbled.

Among tiny shops that lined a narrow street, they found another inn. Again Phineas pounded on the door, and Jabez shouted, "Open to pilgrims who have come for the feast."

The innkeeper peered out through a small opening in the door. His eyes narrowed and he shook his head as he looked from Jabez to Phineas.

Joel put down the basket and sighed. "Where can we go? We have no tent and it is late."

The innkeeper glanced at him. "You are with these men?" He thought for a moment. "Well . . . I will see." Soon the doors of the inn swung open.

Men, women, and children, baskets, bundles, and donkeys crowded the courtyard. In its center was a fountain where people dipped their pitchers. Below it was a trough where animals drank.

The innkeeper led Joel, Jabez, and Phineas up steep, dark steps to a balcony. At the far end of it, the innkeeper opened a door to a small room. "This is all I have," he said.

"It is enough," Jabez told him, smiling.

"Let us eat and sleep," he said, uncovering the basket as soon as the innkeeper had left. "Tomorrow comes soon."

When they had eaten, the dishes in the basket were empty. Lifting the cloth at the bottom of the basket, Joel found only crumbs of bread and a few raisins.

61

"Tomorrow, at sundown, the Passover begins," he said. "Where will we eat the feast?"

Jabez answered, "Phineas and I will be busy. You can find some pilgrim friends and eat the Passover with them."

Joel nodded soberly. He knew he could not go with Jabez and Phineas. They had work to do. But eat the Passover with friends? How could he find them in Jerusalem? Ezra would be with his family at his sister's house. Joel did not know where she lived. And if he found Ezra and his father . . . Joel stirred uneasily. They knew his father had said, "You cannot go." No, it would be better to find someone else from Cana — someone who had not heard his father speak.

Tomorrow I will go to the Temple, Joel decided. My father would want me to go there. I shall tell him all I see and do, when I go home . . . when I go . . .

"After the feast, when it is time to go back to Galilee, I will wait for you here," Joel told Jabez.

Phineas grunted.

"You can return with your friends," said Jabez. "We must stay here for a day or two after the feast."

Jabez and Phineas had gone when Joel waked in the morning. He washed at the fountain and ate the raisins and crumbs in the basket.

He left the empty basket in the room. Hurrying down the steep stairs, he passed through the courtyard to the door of the inn and started for the Temple.

THE FEAST

Outside the inn a crowd of people moved slowly along the narrow street. Joel felt a little frightened.

"Which way is it to the Temple?" he asked a man.

"We are all going there," answered the man. "Follow us."

Joel walked along with other pilgrims, past shops and houses and walls, and past Roman soldiers, standing guard.

At last they reached the market place of the Temple. It was crowded with people. Some were buying doves, spices, incense, and oil. Others were paying their taxes for the Temple. Strangers from many lands were talking in their native languages.

Little by little, Joel edged his way through the market place and into the first court of the Temple. Just in front of him two men were talking together.

"Our law says the Gentiles may not come beyond this court," said one man. "But see!" He pointed to the Fortress Antonia to the north of the Temple. "Roman soldiers stand there and stare down into our holy place."

The other man glanced around fearfully. Then he muttered, "True! They have no right to do that. But speak carefully. We cannot know who is near to listen."

The crowd in back pushed Joel forward. He went up the steps, through a gate in the high wall, and into the Court of the Women.

Near the next court, where only men could go, he saw the family from Nazareth — the tall man, the boy, and his mother. They were speaking together. Then Joel saw the woman walk to the balcony above the entrance.

Last year my mother watched me from there, he thought, when I went with my father into the Court of Israel to become a son of the Law.

Joel remembered the solemn ceremony. He looked around for the man and the boy, but they had disappeared in the crowd.

Climbing the steps, Joel passed into the Court of Israel. He went near the low railing around the sacred, inner place. There was a sound of trumpets and the chanting of psalms. Joel saw the priests in white robes moving back and forth.

" 'Hear, O Israel, the Lord our God is one Lord,' " Joel prayed. He started to repeat the commandments:

" 'I am the Lord thy God . . .
Thou shalt have no other gods before me.' "

When he came to the one: " 'Honor thy father . . .' " Joel lifted his head and glanced around.

Last year his father had stood beside him here in this holy

place. Afterward they had gone to their tent on the hillside, where his mother and Reba had the feast ready. This year . . . he would find the pilgrims from Cana and eat the feast with them. How could he find them among all these people? If he stood on the steps that led from the Court of the Women into the Court of Israel, he could look down at the crowd. That way he would surely see someone from Cana and he could call to them . . .

People came and went as he watched from the top step, but Joel did not see anyone he knew.

I will find them among the tents, he decided. He left the Temple and walked across the bridge to the Mount of Olives.

"Where are the tents of the people from Cana?" he asked.

"Yonder, I think," said a man. But when Joel went where the man pointed, the people there were not from Cana.

Joel asked others. He walked between row after row of tents, looking for someone he knew. Everywhere pilgrims were preparing for the feast. Girls were washing bitter herbs and setting out cups and bowls. Boys were turning the meat which roasted over the little fires that burned before the tents. The smell of cooking meat made Joel hungry. It was growing late, and he still had not found anyone from Cana.

A woman came out of a tent. She looked at Joel and smiled. "I heard footsteps," she said. "I thought you were my son, coming to turn the lamb on the spit."

"I . . . I will turn it," Joel offered.

"Thank you," said the woman, and went back into the tent.

I have seen her before, thought Joel. Then he remembered. She was from Nazareth, the mother of the boy.

Joel turned the meat on the rod over the fire. He could hear the woman moving about inside the tent, setting out food for the feast. In a little while she came out again and stood near him. Looking toward Jerusalem, she murmured, "The Passover begins at sundown. They should come soon." She turned to Joel with a question in her soft, dark eyes. "Your mother will be waiting for you?"

Joel bent his head. "She did not come . . . or my father."

"You are alone?" exclaimed the woman. "Then you must eat with us. See! My son and my husband come now."

When they drew near she told them, "We have a guest."

The boy from Nazareth smiled at his mother and at Joel.

In his deep voice the man said, "You are welcome. You came to Jerusalem for the feast? You are a son of the Law?"

"Yes," answered Joel. His heart was beating fast.

"And your name?" asked the man.

"Joel, the son of Abner the potter, in Cana," he answered.

"We are from Nazareth," said the man. "My name is Joseph. I am a carpenter."

He seated himself by the tray on which the food was placed, and motioned to Joel to do the same.

While they were speaking, the boy from Nazareth lighted the lamp and placed it on the tray. He helped his mother bring the roasted meat from the spit. He brought a pitcher and towel and poured water over his father's hands.

Watching him, Joel thought: He is kind and gentle, like his mother. Strong, too, like his father.

The boy came to pour water over Joel's hands. Joel glanced up into his face. There was something . . . different . . . about this boy from Nazareth.

There was something...different...about this boy from Nazareth

"The Feast of the Passover is ready," said the woman. Softly she started to sing a hymn of praise.

Joseph blessed the wine. The mother passed bitter herbs, with vinegar to dip them in, and dates, and raisins.

Then the boy asked: " 'What mean ye by this service?' "

At home it had been Joel's part to ask that question. It hurt a little when he thought that Zeri would be asking it now.

Joseph gave the solemn answer: " 'It is the sacrifice of the Lord's passover, who passed over the houses of the children of Israel in Egypt, when he smote the Egyptians, and delivered our houses.' "

Joel listened as Joseph repeated the old, old story.

They ate the unleavened bread with the roasted meat. When they had finished, they sang again. The voice of the carpenter was low and rumbling; the woman's voice was soft and sweet; the boy's, rich and clear. At first Joel listened, and then he joined in.

When the woman started to sing: " 'Bless the Lord, O my soul,' " tears came into Joel's eyes and choked his voice. He stopped singing. That was the song his mother sang, almost every day. If he closed his eyes, he could hear her.

The feast was over. Joel did not want to leave, but he knew he should not stay longer. "I must go now," he said. "Thank you . . ." He swallowed hard.

The woman seemed to understand. She smiled and asked, "You have a place to sleep?"

Joel nodded.

" 'The Lord bless thee, and keep thee,' " said Joseph.

The boy from Nazareth stood at the tent door. "Peace," he said quietly as Joel went out.

The pilgrims had stopped singing. The little tents on the hill-side were closed against the night. Everywhere there were silence and darkness.

Joel walked away from the tent. Could he find the way back to the room at the inn? As he stumbled down the hillside, he came to a garden. Gnarled olive trees grew there between great rocks. The leaves rustled softly in the night wind.

I will stay here, Joel decided. Close to a big rock he lay down.

"Peace." The word the boy of Nazareth had spoken echoed in Joel's heart. Falling asleep, he dreamed he was home, in Cana.

Trumpet blasts from the Temple awakened Joel. The sun was rising. He hurried to the Temple.

Priests in white robes were busy at the altar. Joel saw a wisp and then a cloud of sweet smoke rise above the holy place where the priests were burning incense.

Today I will find the pilgrims from Cana, thought Joel when the morning sacrifices were over. They must be here in the Temple.

He walked in and out among the people, looking for them. He saw a man and a woman bringing their first-born son to the Temple. He saw a proud-looking man, in a fringed robe, standing for a long time as he prayed. Near the Beautiful Gate Joel saw the poor people, the blind, and the crippled, begging from those who passed by.

I would give to them if I had anything to give, he thought.

He remembered the coin the Roman soldier had thrown to him, and searched through the folds of his waistband. Yes, it was still there, and his knife. But he could not give the coin away. It was all he had to buy food, until he found some of his friends.

From the Temple, Joel wandered into the market place. Perhaps someone from Cana might be there.

As he stood beside a scribe, watching him write a letter, Joel heard a man shouting. "What is that?" he asked.

Without lifting his head, the scribe answered, "Someone trying to stir the people to rebellion against the Romans."

Joel pushed his way through the crowd until he stood close to the man who was shouting.

"The God of our fathers will send his Anointed One to rule over us." The dark eyes of the man gleamed fiercely as he looked up at the Fortress Antonia. He shook his fist. "Throw out the Romans! Send their soldiers back over the sea!"

Joel stared at the man with admiration. This man was not afraid of the Romans. He was a patriot. If only his father and the people of Cana were here to see him!

Suddenly a bugle sounded. People scattered. But before everyone could get away, soldiers rushed in. They surrounded the man who had been shouting and a few others near him, including Joel.

"Take them to the dungeon in the Tower of Antonia," a tall young officer, a centurion, commanded.

"No," cried Joel. "NO!" He tried to break his way through the guard. A soldier pushed him back.

The centurion eyed him sharply. "Is your father here among the prisoners?" he asked.

Joel could not speak. He shook his head.

"He is only a boy. Let him go," ordered the centurion. "But take the others."

Joel's heart was pounding. Where could he go to be safe? Where but in the Temple! He did not stop until he stood in the

Court of Israel. There he looked up at the Tower of Antonia. He saw the Roman guards pacing back and forth. Their brass helmets and breastplates glistened in the sun. Their spears looked sharp.

What if they had taken him and thrown him into a dark dungeon and locked the door? His family would never have known where he was. No one would have come to help him.

A cold chill touched Joel's face. He must find his friends . . . he must find the pilgrims from Cana.

STARTING HOME

After a while, when the thumping in his chest quieted, Joel walked about the Temple again, looking for some familiar face. He felt small and alone, and hungry. He would have to go to the lower part of the city to buy food.

Fearfully, he ventured out of the Temple. In a little shop he asked for bread and milk and handed the shopkeeper the coin the Roman had thrown to him.

The man glanced at the coin. He gave Joel a bowl of milk and part of a loaf of bread, and handed him back several small coins. Joel put them carefully away. They would buy food until he found someone from Cana. Or perhaps here in the city he might meet Jabez and Phineas.

Munching the bread, Joel walked up and down the narrow city streets, hoping to see someone he knew. Looking, too, for the inn.

Evening came. The Feast of the Passover was ended. Joel had not found the inn, or anyone from Cana, or Jabez and Phineas. Discouraged and weary, he went back to the garden to sleep.

Tomorrow, he said to himself, I will surely find the pilgrims from Cana. They will be starting home and I will go with them. What will my father say when I reach home?

Early in the morning there was much stirring about on the hillside. Pilgrims were loading their donkeys and carts. They were going home.

Joel went from group to group, looking everywhere for the people from Cana. When he grew tired he sat on a wall overlooking the road. Someone he knew must come soon. Perhaps it would be Ezra! Joel smiled, thinking how surprised his friend would be to see him. It would be fun to walk with Ezra — better even than to walk with Jabez and Phineas. Ezra and he could go together all the way to Cana . . . home. A tightness grew inside him when he thought of home, and of his father.

Afternoon came. No one from Cana had passed.

I must start back alone, Joel decided. But first I will buy food for my journey. I will get as much bread as I can for my coins.

He jumped from the wall, walked over the bridge, through the Temple, and down to the crowded market place. There he met an old man with a tray of bread. "Bread, freshly baked," he was crying in a shrill, cracked voice.

Joel took the coins from his waistband and held them in his hand. "How much can I buy — " he began.

Just then two slaves pushed their way through the crowd in the narrow street. "Make way! Make way!" they shouted.

73

People scrambled to one side and the other, knocking Joel against the old man and tumbling some of the bread off the tray.

Two young men followed the slaves through the opening they had made in the crowd. They wore fine white turbans and robes of purple silk. Gold chains hung around their necks.

"Who are they?" Joel asked the old man, as he helped him to pick up the bread.

"Rich men's sons," muttered the old man. "Brought up in Rome, they do as the Romans do. They spend their time watching chariot races and gladiators fighting wild beasts." He shook his head. "You wanted to buy bread? Where is your money?"

"Money!" Joel looked at his empty hands. "It . . . it is gone!"

The old man shrugged. "Bread . . . fresh bread," he called and moved on.

Joel picked up some broken pieces of bread from the ground and tucked them in his waistband. He tried to see his lost coins between the feet of the people who were passing. Reaching down, he bumped into a stranger.

"Look where you go!" the man cried angrily and rapped Joel on the head.

Someone stepped on his fingers as he felt in the dust, trying to find his coins. But the coins had disappeared. He could not find even one.

How could he buy food for the gnawing emptiness in his stomach, and for the journey home? He thought of the bread his mother baked and the stews she cooked. His throat ached. Cana was three days' journey away.

He put his bruised fingers on his knife. Would he have to sell that to buy food?

Upset and unhappy, Joel walked back through the Temple. At a fountain he stopped to drink and to bathe his sore fingers. He crossed the bridge from the Temple to the Mount of Olives on his way to the garden.

Passing under a fig tree, he glanced up and saw some of the tender buds that came before the true figs. He climbed up and gathered them. In the garden he took the pieces of bread from his waistband, brushed off the dust, and ate the bread and the fig buds.

The hillside was strangely bare and quiet now that the pilgrims had gone.

I should have gone too, Joel said to himself. Many of them would go as far as Beth-shan. From there I could have followed the highway home. Somewhere along the way I might have found the people from Cana . . .

But when Joel thought of his father, he decided that it was too late for him to start that day.

"I will go . . . tomorrow," he said aloud.

In the morning Joel tightened his waistband. He took out his knife and looked at it. He did not want to part with it, but how else could he get food for his journey? If only he knew where Jabez and Phineas were! He had shared the food in the basket with them — the meat and the little salted fish. They would help him, if they knew he was hungry. Most likely they were still in Jerusalem. Jabez had said they would stay a day or two after the feast.

Where can I find them? Joel asked himself, looking thoughtfully toward the city. If I walk through the narrow, twisting streets, I will miss them . . . just as I missed the people from Cana.

"I could stand on the bridge that leads from the Temple to the highway," he murmured. "They will be sure to leave Jerusalem

75

that way . . ." He put his knife away. "I will wait for them there," he said.

Many people crossed the bridge, going and coming — merchants with loaded donkeys and carts, farmers bringing fruits and vegetables, a shepherd leading his flock of sheep.

Joel saw a farmer leave the crowd and go to the stream that flowed beneath the bridge. The farmer emptied his basket of vegetables onto the ground and sorted them. He put some back into his deep, round basket. Others, he tossed away. When his basket was arranged, he lifted it to his back, trudged up the hillside, crossed the bridge, and passed into the city, going to the market place.

There was no shade on the bridge. The sun was bright and hot. Joel wondered how long he would have to wait. If only he had something to eat! As he grew hungrier he began to think of the vegetables the farmer had thrown aside.

For a while he hesitated, afraid to leave the bridge, afraid he might miss Jabez and Phineas. But it was the middle of the day. Only a few people were crossing the bridge just then, and he would hurry.

Down where the farmer had been, Joel lifted the bottom of his cloak and quickly gathered into it the vegetables strewn on the ground.

He climbed up the hillside and squatted at one side of the bridge. There he looked over what he had picked up — greens that had wilted, beans that were spotted, broken leeks, a few lentils. Joel ate everything he could, and felt better.

The day was passing. He grew anxious. What if Jabez and Phineas did not come today . . . or tomorrow?

Late in the afternoon Joel saw two men come through the

Many people crossed the bridge

gate of the Temple and start across the bridge. There was something familiar about them. His heart gave a jump.

"Jabez! Phineas!" Joel called out and ran toward them.

"I . . . waited . . . for you," he said, out of breath.

Jabez frowned. "Why did you not go with your friends?"

"I did not find them," answered Joel.

Jabez looked at him shrewdly. "You have nothing? No money, no food for your journey?"

Phineas growled, half under his breath, "Let us go."

Joel spoke quickly. "I can buy food. I can sell my knife." He showed it to Jabez.

"Where did you get that?" snapped Jabez. He started to take it, then stopped.

"I found it in a cave," answered Joel. He tucked the knife in his waistband.

Jabez and Phineas looked at each other for a moment.

"We are in a hurry," said Jabez, starting on. "We must walk fast."

"I will walk fast too," said Joel, following them.

It was hard for him to keep up with the men, and the way they had looked at each other gave him an uneasy feeling. But he was glad to see someone he knew, glad to be on his way home. He had been gone a long while. He counted the days. Seven! Even if his father punished him, he would be glad to get home.

They followed the highway around the Mount of Olives, and past Bethany. It was dusk when they paused at the spring, En Shemish, to drink.

Joel wished he could stop there and rest, but Jabez and Phineas were going on. Wearily, he went along. Somehow his legs would not move as fast as he wanted them to.

Beyond the spring there was a bend in the road.

"Phineas and I are stopping here to sleep," said Jabez.

It was a lonely spot. Joel looked around. Where else could he go? "I will sleep here too," he said.

With Jabez and Phineas he climbed the steep bank of a rocky, treeless hill. They sat down, and Jabez opened a bundle. In it there were bread and cheese. He broke a large piece of bread for Phineas and handed him the cheese. He gave Joel a piece of bread, too, with a little cheese. The rest he kept for himself.

Joel ate greedily. He could have eaten more, but there was no more. He folded his cloak about him and lay down. They had started late and they had walked fast. Another night, two more days, and he would be home! He thought of his mother, Reba, and Zeri, and wondered again what his father would say . . .

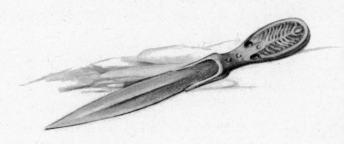

THIEVES!

Suddenly, in the night, Joel awoke. Was he dreaming — or had he really heard voices?

He jumped up. In the light of the rising moon he saw two men run down the highway and disappear behind a low hill. Two men . . . like Jabez and Phineas.

Joel rubbed his eyes and looked around for them. They were not there. He was alone. "They went away and left me," he whispered.

The night air was cool. As he wrapped his cloak closer about him, he missed the hard feel of his knife. His waistband was loose. He searched every fold. His knife was gone!

"Someone took it while I slept," he whispered. Joel remembered the way Jabez had looked at it. "Jabez?" he muttered.

Was that a cry? Joel listened. From the road came the sound of a man's voice. "Help!"

Joel slid down the hill. Below it, a man was lying in the road. Kneeling beside him, Joel asked, "What happened? Are you hurt . . . hurt badly?"

"Thieves," groaned the man. "I met the same two in the market place today. They saw I had money. They heard my plans and came and lay in wait for me. They took all I had."

Two men! Joel caught his breath. Jabez and Phineas?

The man groaned again. "My leg is hurt and my arm gashed. One of the men had a knife."

My knife! thought Joel. He helped the man tear a strip of cloth from his undergarment and bind up his wound.

"I cannot continue my journey," said the man. "I must return to Jerusalem. Help me to stand."

He leaned heavily on Joel's shoulder. Step by step they made their way back to the spring.

"I can walk no farther," said the man with a sigh.

Joel drew water for him to drink and helped him wash the blood from his arm. The man groaned with the pain. He lay down, and Joel sat beside him, thinking of his knife that was gone and of Jabez and Phineas. They were not patriots! They were wicked men . . . thieves! Over and over the words whispered themselves inside him . . . wicked men . . . thieves!

"As soon as it is light," the man was saying to Joel, "go to Jerusalem for me. Go to the shop of my friend, Eban the sandal maker. Tell him all that has happened. Ask him to bring men and a litter to carry me. You will find his shop a few streets beyond the Temple. Ask for Eban. Many people know him. I have no money now, alas, but Eban will pay you."

"I will go," said Joel.

His heart and his feet felt heavy as he walked back to Jerusalem instead of hurrying on toward Cana. The sun was high before he found Eban's shop, and delivered the message.

"My friend robbed! Wounded!" cried Eban.

Joel nodded and blinked his eyes. He was tired, and everything seemed to be spinning around. He put out his hand to steady himself by touching the doorpost of the shop. Then he sat down suddenly on the stone floor.

"Sarah!" shouted Eban. "Sarah!"

A short, stout woman came from the back of the shop, asking in a calm voice, "What is it, my husband?"

"This boy brings a message," said Eban. In quick, excited words he repeated what Joel had told him. "I must go," he said. "I must go at once. My friend! my poor friend!"

"He said you would pay me," Joel began. Eban did not seem to hear.

Talking to himself and shaking his head, Eban hurried away.

Joel started to get up, but his legs were shaky. In a moment he felt a cool hand on his forehead.

"What happened to you?" asked Sarah in a kindly tone. "Were you hurt, too?"

Joel shook his head. "I am tired . . . and . . . and . . ."

The woman interrupted. "You are hungry! Rest here. I will bring you something to eat." She came back with a bowl of warm goat's milk, and Joel drank it eagerly. She filled it again and brought him bread and cheese and dates.

While Joel ate, Sarah moved quietly about the shop. She put away the tools Eban had dropped and talked to Joel. "Thieves and outlaws hide in the hills. No one should walk there alone after

82

dark. It is not safe." She looked at Joel. "How did it happen you were there?"

He answered slowly, "I came to Jerusalem for the feast. I was on my way home . . . to Galilee."

"Galilee!" exclaimed Sarah. "That is far. And you came alone?"

Joel shook his head. "I came . . . I mean, I could not find my friends."

"You lost them," said Sarah with a sigh. "That is how it is when the great crowds come for the feasts." She hung up a pair of sandals Eban had tossed aside. "You were on your way home and came all the way back to bring the message?"

"Yes," answered Joel.

Sarah turned quickly. "Eban was to pay you. And he would.

83

But you have a long way to go. You will not want to wait for his return. And I have no money," she murmured, looking thoughtful. "I could give you some f[ ]d to take with you. Come! I will get it ready."

Joel followed her to the room back of the shop. There he rested while the woman packed a small round basket with bread and cheese, olives and dates.

She handed it to him with a warm smile. "Now be sure to find other travelers going your way. Do not walk alone on the highway at night."

"Thank you," said Joel. He took the basket and moved slowly away. If he started now, how far could he get before it grew dark? He had not slept much during the night . . . he was so tired.

He lay down beside the rock in the garden and fell asleep.

It was evening when he awoke and sat up. He looked for his little basket. It was safe beside him. He heard footsteps. Someone was coming! Could it be Jabez and Phineas?

Joel sighed with relief when he saw that it was a man and a woman walking past.

"Where can he be?" he heard the woman ask.

Joel could not hear what the man answered, but there was strength and comfort in the sound of his voice. It made Joel think of his father . . .

He knew the pilgrims from Cana would be home soon. His father would ask them about him. Everyone in the village would know that he had gone away, disobeying his father. What would they think? What would his father and mother think?

Joel thought of the day his father had told him to stay in the shop and he had gone away and taken Zeri. He remembered his father's tone as he said, "You have disobeyed. Do not let it happen again."

But it had happened again. And this time he had gone away and stayed a long time. Even worse, he had eaten and walked and slept with thieves. Jabez and Phineas were not patriots. They were thieves! He had brought dishonor to his father.

Sick at heart, Joel twisted and turned. It was long before he slept again.

Temple trumpets and crowing cocks woke him. He covered his face with his cloak and lay thinking. He knew he should start at once for Cana. It would be a long walk and a lonely one. Dangerous, too. In the barren hills, beyond the spring, thieves might lie in wait. Jabez and Phineas themselves, perhaps.

He wished he had never met them. His father had said, "Walk as far as the highway." If only he had turned back there! If only he had left Ezra and gone home! His father needed him . . . and he needed his father. But when his father knew about Jabez and Phineas, would he . . .

Joel got up and took his basket. He would go to the Temple to pray. Then he would start for home.

IN THE TEMPLE

As Joel walked down the hillside he passed a tent, with a donkey tethered outside. He remembered the man and woman who passed the garden in the night. They must have slept there.

He crossed the bridge to the Temple and entered the Porch of Solomon. Part way down the long colonnade he saw a group of gray-bearded men, teachers of the Law. One of them asked a question. The others leaned forward to listen. A clear, boyish voice answered.

Joel paused and stared. An old one asks questions and a young one answers? He walked nearer to listen and to see.

A boy stood in the center of the group of teachers, a boy about his own age. The boy moved and lifted his head to answer another question. It was the boy from Nazareth! Joel caught his breath, then stepped nearer.

A gray-bearded teacher glanced up. His keen eyes seemed to ask Joel: *What are you doing here?*

Joel hesitated, turned, and went away, into the Temple.

As he walked through the Court of the Gentiles, toward the Court of the Women, he felt a gentle hand on his arm.

"You are the boy who shared the Feast of the Passover with us," said the woman. "Do you remember my son?"

"Yes," answered Joel. "Yes . . . I remember."

Tears filled the woman's eyes. "He is lost," she said. "We thought he was with our company. We went a day's journey before we missed him." She glanced up at the tall, kindly man beside her. "For three days now we have searched . . ."

Joel interrupted. "He is not lost! I saw him, just now, talking with the teachers of the Law."

Joseph spoke. "You are sure?"

"I will take you to him," Joel said with eagerness, and led the way to the Porch of Solomon.

When the woman saw the boy, she hurried forward with a glad cry. Joseph followed her.

Joel walked after them part way. He stopped beside a great white pillar, watching and listening.

The gray-bearded men sat silent as the woman spoke to the boy: "Son, why have you treated us so? Your father and I have been looking for you anxiously."

For a moment the boy seemed puzzled. "How is it that you sought me?" he asked. A shaft of sunshine between the pillars lighted his face and he smiled. "Did you not know that I must be in my Father's house?"

His Father's house? thought Joel, leaning against the pillar. I know . . . he means this house, the Temple!

Several of the teachers were speaking at the same time. Joel

could not hear all they said. Were they urging the boy not to go? Would he stay with them? No . . . he was bidding them good-by and leaving with his mother and father.

As they came toward the pillar where he stood, Joel looked intently at the boy. His face and his eyes were shining. As though, thought Joel, he had a lighted lamp inside. And there was something . . . something more . . . about the boy from Nazareth.

Joel longed to reach out and touch him. He wanted to speak to him. Instead, he slipped back of the pillar where he could not be seen. They were so happy together — the boy and his mother and father!

When they had passed, Joel followed until they left the Porch of Solomon. Then he walked slowly through the Temple to the inner court, the Court of Israel.

He could still see the glowing face of the Nazareth boy who stayed in his Father's house . . . the Temple.

Joel bowed his head. The priests were chanting:

" 'The Lord is merciful and gracious,
   Slow to anger and abounding in steadfast love.
   As far as the east is from the west,
   So far does he remove our transgressions from us.
   As a father pities his children,
   So the Lord pities those who fear him.' "

The words of the psalm seemed to be speaking to Joel.

"Like as a father," he whispered. Would his father forgive him? He thought of the boy from Nazareth, going home with his mother and father.

Joel took a deep breath. "I am going home, too . . . to my father."

As Joel crossed the bridge, from the Temple to the Mount of Olives, he looked toward the place where he had seen the donkey and the tent. They were gone! The family from Nazareth had already started.

I will follow them, Joel decided. I will not be afraid on the road, if they are near.

Carrying his little basket of food, he slipped in and out among donkeys, carts, and people on the road. He hurried along the way he knew the family from Nazareth must go — past Bethany, the spring, and into the barren hills.

He felt a little anxious about thieves. Men like Jabez and Phineas might be hiding in these hills. But somewhere, on this same highway, the boy from Nazareth was walking with his mother and father. It was a comforting thought to Joel. He scanned the road ahead and tried to walk faster.

Toward dusk he passed through Jericho. It was almost dark

when he saw some people pitching a tent a little way off the road. Joel gave a sigh of relief. It was the family from Nazareth.

Not far away, Joel found some low-growing shrubs. When he had eaten, he crept under the branches to sleep.

A braying donkey woke him in the morning. He rolled from beneath the branches to stretch and yawn. Already there were people on the highway. Farmers were going to their fields, and the family from Nazareth was starting.

At a little distance Joel followed them. He glanced at other travelers on the road and remembered how he had walked along here with Jabez and Phineas . . . how someone had cried "Thieves!" His face burned. "And I thought they were patriots!" he said aloud.

The day grew hot. Several times when he crossed a little stream, he stopped for a quick drink. Then he would walk fast until he could see ahead of him again the tall carpenter from Nazareth, the woman on the donkey, and the boy.

That evening the family from Nazareth opened their tent near some others, between the road and the Jordan River.

Before he came to the tents, Joel walked to the river. He bathed his dusty feet and sat down under a palm tree. While he was eating, he fell asleep.

Morning sounds woke him. The people in the tents had gone. Joel started on his way. He trudged along the road behind the family from Nazareth.

The highway led through the Gap of Jezreel, across the Jordan River and through the city of Beth-shan, past the inn. What if the innkeeper there should see him and remember that he had come with Jabez and Phineas? Joel bent his head and hurried by.

At the edge of the city, he passed a carpenter's shop. He paused a moment to rest and to watch a man making a plow. The father of the boy from Nazareth was a carpenter, too, Joel remembered. Did the boy work with him in his shop and make things of wood with saw and hammer and chisel?

I am going to make things, too, Joel said to himself as he went on. I will be a potter, like my father.

Beside the road he found a little patch of ripening grain. He pulled some of the heads, crushed the hulls, and ate the kernels. There was not much food left in the basket. He would save it for later . . .

He came to the place where the boy from Nazareth had passed him and spoken . . . "Peace!" . . . and where Phineas had grabbed him. Soon he would come to the spot where he had found the basket, near the Nazareth road.

The Nazareth road! The family from Nazareth would leave the highway there to walk south. He would go on — on to Cana, and home.

The half light of early evening, and dust from the road, had almost hidden the tall carpenter, his wife and the boy when Joel reached the Nazareth road. He stood on the highway, looking with longing down the hill, thinking of the boy . . . hoping to see him again.

"Peace," whispered Joel. But he did not feel peaceful inside. Tired and forlorn, he plodded on, almost alone on the highway.

HOME, IN CANA

When Joel reached the Cana road, he sat down to rest and to eat the last of his food. Below him, beyond the tiny lights of a village, was his father's house. What were they doing? he wondered. Reba would have gone to the fountain. Zeri would have brought in the goat. His mother would be taking the bread from the oven, and his father . . . alone in the shop! Would he be . . . treading? Joel took a deep breath.

He remembered the words of the carpenter's wife when she found her son. "We have been looking for you anxiously." Had his mother and father been anxious about him?

Brushing the sleeve of his cloak across his face, Joel started down the road. The moon rose as he walked. It shone upon white stone walls and houses. He passed through a village and walked on and on to Cana.

The gate to his father's home was only half shut. Joel slipped through it. Moonlight flooded the courtyard. Everything was so still, he could hear the thumping of his heart!

They are all asleep, he decided. My father, too. What shall I say to him? I will wait until morning.

Joel felt his way into the dark workshop, lay down on the floor, and slept.

When it began to grow light, he sat up and blinked the sleep from his eyes. He glanced around the shop. So few pots and jars waiting to be fired? He got up and put his foot on a pile of clay. How queer that it was dry!

Any moment now his father would come.

I will tell him about the basket, and how I met . . . No! Joel shook his head. How could he tell his father about Jabez and Phineas?

There was the rattle of the chain around the goat's neck and the sound of hoofs on the stones in the courtyard. Joel held his breath and listened. That would be Zeri, leading out the goat!

I will go with Zeri, Joel decided quickly. When we return, my father will be here in the shop. Then I will tell him where I have been . . . and all that happened.

Quietly Joel crossed the courtyard and followed Zeri out the gate and up the path.

His little brother glanced back. "Joel!" He dropped the chain and rushed to throw his arms about Joel. "You were away so long!"

Joel picked up the chain and started toward the field.

"We thought you went to Jerusalem," Zeri said as they walked on. "But Ezra and Hiram came home, and you were not with them. And all the other pilgrims came, too, and you were not with them. Mother and Reba cried. We did not know what had happened to

Joel tried to speak, but no words came

you. Then Father said he would find you." Zeri smiled up at Joel. "Father brought you home."

Joel shook his head. "I came alone."

"Then where is Father?" asked Zeri. His dark eyes grew wide. "He went to Tyre . . ."

"Father! To Tyre!" exclaimed Joel.

Zeri nodded. "Because you wanted to go with Simon. Father thought you had gone there. He went to look for you."

"I have not seen him," said Joel in a low choked voice.

They reached the field. Joel fastened the goat's chain around the stump of the tree.

Zeri held Joel's hand tightly and talked as they went home. Joel did not listen. His mother and Reba had cried. His father had gone all the way to Tyre to look for him . . .

"There comes Father now," cried Zeri. "See?"

"Go tell Mother I have come," said Joel. "I will meet Father." His voice sounded strange to him. He walked a little way, stopped, and dug his toes into the dusty path.

Abner's steps were slow and heavy. There was a droop to his shoulders, and tired lines in his face. Had he walked all night? Joel's throat grew tight. All the brave words he had planned to speak washed away from his mind, like little stones from the clay.

Abner lifted his head. He came quickly and put his hand on Joel's shoulder. "Joel!"

The touch, the tone brought an ache within Joel's heart. He tried to speak, but at first no words came. He swallowed hard, and whispered, "I . . . I disobeyed."

"Yes," said his father, with sadness. "You brought sorrow to your mother and to me."

Joel looked down. Sorrow? What would his father say when he knew about Jabez and Phineas? He knew now he had to tell him that part, too.

"I . . . met two men. I went to Jerusalem with them. They . . ." Joel paused. It was hard to say the words. "They were . . . thieves."

"Thieves!" exclaimed his father in a shocked tone. He stood silent for a moment. When he spoke, his deep voice trembled. "The clay is often stubborn, but the Master Potter is patient. 'The Lord is merciful . . . and gracious!'"

"Merciful and gracious!" The words of the psalm echoed through Joel's mind:

> " 'As far as the east is from the west,
> So far does he remove our transgressions from us.
> As a father . . .' "

"You have come home," said his father.

Joel looked up. He saw forgiveness and love in his father's eyes.

"Home!" said Joel softly. All the old restlessness was gone. *Peace!* . . . the word the boy of Nazareth had spoken, flowed into Joel's heart.